PUFFIN BOOKS

The Worst Witch Saves the Day

Jill Murphy started putting books together (literally with a stapler), when she was six. Her Worst Witch series, the first of which was published in 1975, is hugely successful. She has also written and illustrated several award-winning picture books for younger children.

Books by Jill Murphy

(Titles in reading order)

THE WORST WITCH
THE WORST WITCH STRIKES AGAIN
A BAD SPELL FOR THE WORST WITCH
THE WORST WITCH ALL AT SEA
THE WORST WITCH SAVES THE DAY

Praise for *The Worst Witch Saves the Day*

'Hurray for Jill Murphy . . . little girls will love the antics of
Mildred Hubble and her hopeless tabby cat' – *Independent*

'Millions of young readers have fallen under the spell of
Jill Murphy's *Worst Witch*'
– *Sunday Express*

'A lovely, sparky book' – *Observer*

'Mildred Hubble makes a welcome return' – *Guardian*

'Witty and original' – *Books for Keeps*

JILL MURPHY

THE
Worst Witch
SAVES THE DAY

PUFFIN

PUFFIN BOOKS

Published by the Penguin Group
Penguin Books Ltd, 80 Strand, London WC2R 0RL, England
Penguin Group (USA) Inc., 375 Hudson Street, New York, New York 10014, USA
Penguin Group (Canada), 90 Eglinton Avenue East, Suite 700, Toronto, Ontario, Canada M4P 2Y3
(a division of Pearson Penguin Canada Inc.)
Penguin Ireland, 25 St Stephen's Green, Dublin 2, Ireland (a division of Penguin Books Ltd)
Penguin Group (Australia), 250 Camberwell Road, Camberwell, Victoria 3124, Australia
(a division of Pearson Australia Group Pty Ltd)
Penguin Books India Pvt Ltd, 11 Community Centre, Panchsheel Park, New Delhi - 110 017, India
Penguin Group (NZ), cnr Airborne and Rosedale Roads, Albany, Auckland 1310, New Zealand
(a division of Pearson New Zealand Ltd)
Penguin Books (South Africa) (Pty) Ltd, 24 Sturdee Avenue, Rosebank, Johannesburg 2196, South Africa

Penguin Books Ltd, Registered Offices: 80 Strand, London WC2R 0RL, England

penguin.com

First published 2005
Published in this edition 2006
6

Copyright © Jill Murphy, 2005
All rights reserved

The moral right of the author/illustrator has been asserted

Set in Baskerville
Made and printed in England by Clays Ltd, St Ives plc

British Library Cataloguing in Publication Data
A CIP catalogue record for this book is available from the British Library

ISBN-13: 978-0-141-31434-1
ISBN-10: 0-141-31434-6

This book belongs
to

Lucy Desmulliez

CHAPTER ONE

Tropical sunshine beat down on the pupils of Miss Cackle's Academy for Witches as they arrived in the schoolyard on the first day of Winter Term. Only the first-years entered the school on foot, as they had not learnt to fly yet, but all the other pupils, and of course the teachers, soared over the high stone wall on their broomsticks like a flock of crows – a spectacular sight to see. The school year was divided into two long terms, instead of the usual three, so the weather conditions were often mismatched to the girls' uniforms at the very beginning of term.

'This is just typical!' thought Mildred Hubble, wriggling her toes uncomfortably inside thick grey socks and heavy winter boots. 'When we came back for Summer Term it was snowing and we were all frozen to death in our summer dresses!'

Mildred was beginning her third year at Miss Cackle's Academy. She was relieved to be coming back at all, after an accident-prone two years under the beady eye of the blood-curdling Miss Hardbroom (or H.B. as the girls called her), who had been Mildred's form-mistress for both of those years. However, this term Mildred felt much more confident. During the summer break, she had been on a special two-week broomstick crash course (a rather unfortunate description in Mildred's case) and had received a Broomstick Proficiency Certificate and a smart new broom from her mum as a reward. Sadly, her cat, Tabby, who was the only tabby cat in the school (all the rest being regulation black ones), had not improved very much – in fact, at *all*, if one was to be truthful. Of course he had got *used* to flying

after four terms' practice, but he still
hated it and always crouched down on
the back of the broom in a guinea-pig-
like hunch, or, worse, completely flat
so that he could hang on better.

However, he was a very affectionate
and cuddly cat, just the sort to curl up
with on a freezing night at the
stone-built, draughty school, and
Mildred loved him with all her heart.

Mildred zipped over the school wall without wobbling, despite the heavy luggage hanging from the back, and coasted to a halt near the broom shed.

'Not bad, Mildred Hubble,' said a sneery voice from the gloomy interior. 'Had a brain transplant during the hols, did you?'

'Oh, hello, Ethel,' said Mildred without enthusiasm, as she peered in and saw who it was. Ethel Hallow was the top student in Mildred's class. She was brilliant at every subject, including popularity with the teachers, which had unfortunately gone to her head and given her a tendency to belittle her classmates. Mildred's lack of ability in all directions had made her Ethel's number-one target since their very first term.

Mildred unhooked her luggage and clipped her broomstick into the rack below her name. It always pleased her to see her name waiting for her at the beginning of a new year, above her coat-peg and broomstick-clip and on her bedroom door, as if everyone expected her to come back as a matter of course. 'Mildred Hubble' it proclaimed, as if she was important in the world.

'Nice broom,' said Ethel. 'Pity to waste it on someone like you.'

'Don't *start*, Ethel,' warned Mildred.

'Start *what*?' exclaimed Ethel loudly in an innocent tone. 'Honestly, Mildred Hubble, you're so touchy.'

Mildred made her way out into the yard and scanned the groups of girls for one of her friends.

'Maud – is that you?' she called, as she suddenly realized that the smiling person running towards her was her best friend, with her hair in curly bunches instead of the usual straight ones.

'Of course it's me,' laughed Maud. 'Do you like the hairdo? My aunt gave me a brilliant styling brush. You just turn it on for a bit, roll up your hair in it and – Abracadabra! – your hair's all curly. You can have a go if you like.'

'Thanks, Maudy,' said Mildred. 'Oh, it's *so* nice to see you again. It's the only thing that makes this school worthwhile, knowing you're in it with me.'

'Well, I'm not going anywhere else for the next several years!' said Maud. 'So we're well and truly in it together – as long as you don't go and get yourself expelled.'

'No chance,' said Mildred. 'I'm going to be the best witch in the world this term, just you wait and see. Look, isn't that Enid landing by the wall? And there's the bell. Let's go and see who we've got this year. It can't be H.B. *again!*'

CHAPTER TWO

It wasn't H.B., much to Form Three's utter joy. It was a new teacher, named Miss Granite. 'Welcome, girls,' said Miss Cackle, smiling fondly at her flock of pupils, all lined up in orderly rows in the yard. 'I hope you've all had a wonderful summer holiday and are rested and ready for some hard work, especially our new pupils. Don't worry, girls, it won't be long before you're all doing loop-the-loops around the bell-tower!'

Miss Hardbroom raised a disapproving eyebrow at Miss Cackle's light-hearted attempt at friendliness, and the new girls looked more anxious than ever as they were not sure whether to laugh or to look serious. Although Miss Cackle was the headmistress of Miss Cackle's Academy, Miss Hardbroom had somehow risen through the ranks of the teachers to be an unofficial second-in-command who seemed more in charge than the headmistress. Because of this, the girls were always caught nervously between Miss Cackle's kindliness and Miss Hardbroom's overriding disapproval. Miss Cackle gave up her attempt at joviality and handed the morning over to Miss Hardbroom.

'Now then, everyone,' she said, in a rather crestfallen voice, 'I'll leave it to Miss Hardbroom to introduce our new form-teacher and to give out any announcements before you go and unpack your belongings. I'll see you all at assembly afterwards.'

'Thank you, Miss Cackle,' said Miss Hardbroom, with a nod in the headmistress's direction as the girls all stood in line, gasping in the heat. 'Now then, Form Three, this is your new form-mistress, Miss Granite – put your hat back on, Enid Nightshade, it isn't *that* hot. Goodness me, you're all so feeble these days – always complaining about something. Either it's too hot or it's too cold. No backbone at all, no gumption.'

Miss Granite gave a little cough.

'Ah, yes, girls,' continued Miss Hardbroom. 'Please greet Miss Granite in a courteous and friendly manner.'

'Good *morning*, Miss Granite!' chanted the whole class, trying to sound courteous and friendly.

As Miss Hardbroom gave out various announcements, Form Three gazed in amazement at their new form-mistress. She was very strange-looking. For a start, she had a huge cloud of bright-orange curls, which looked extremely frivolous for Miss Cackle's Academy. In fact, everything about Miss Granite looked frivolous to the pupils, condemned as they were to black gymslips, thick wool socks and hobnailed boots. She wore enormous purple-tinted glasses and a short cape with a collar turned up so high that you couldn't see much of her face at all.

'She looks as if she's been at your styling brush,' whispered Mildred to Maud, who giggled.

'Mildred Hubble! If you have something amusing to say, perhaps you could share your little joke with the rest of us,' snapped Miss Hardbroom. 'I'm sure we could *all* do with a little merriment on the first day of this long Winter Term.'

'Sorry, Miss Hardbroom,' mumbled Mildred, blushing scarlet as the rows of assembled girls, plus all the teachers, turned to look at her.

'Well, Mildred,' said Miss Hardbroom. 'We're all waiting.'

'I've forgotten!' said Mildred desperately. 'It probably wasn't all that funny anyway. I really can't remember.'

Miss Hardbroom turned to Miss Granite. '*This* is Mildred Hubble,' she announced. 'It's a bad sign when she can't remember anything on the very first day of term, before lessons have even started. This, I might add, is typical of Mildred Hubble and you would do well to keep an eye on her.'

At this point the girls heard Miss Granite's voice for the first time. It was so astonishingly high-pitched and squeaky that it was hard for them not to react, and even Ethel looked startled.

'Oh, I will, Miss Hardbroom,' squeaked Miss Granite. 'I most certainly will.'

Mildred glanced at Enid and the two of them suddenly felt a dreadful surge of hysteria. Maud gave Mildred a severe look as her friend grimaced with the effort of not bursting into giggles.

'Stop it, Mil,' she whispered. 'Don't get off on the wrong foot with this one. It's your chance to make a fresh start.'

CHAPTER THREE

The girls set off to put their suitcases and cats into their rooms and to get themselves tidied up before assembly, which was held in the Great Hall. Mildred was delighted to find that she now had six bats roosting along her picture rail, instead of the usual three. She was mad about animals and, although the bats didn't do very much except sleep all day – occasionally stretching a wing or shuffling along a bit – it was nice to know they were there. In the early hours, when Mildred was often lying awake worrying about a looming potion test or some similar horror, it was always comforting to see her little flock come in from their night's hunting and jostle into position upside down.

It only took a few minutes for Mildred to unpack her suitcase and put away her clothes, so she decided to nip along the corridor to Maud's room.

'Have you got that styling brush, Maud?' she asked, letting herself in through the heavy oak door. 'I'd like to have a little twirl with it and see if I can liven up my hair a bit.'

Maud was still cramming her clothes into her tiny wardrobe. All the pupils had a wardrobe, with space on one side for their robes and shirts and a narrow set of drawers on the other side, which was not big enough to take a term's supply of socks and underclothes and was, therefore, very difficult to keep tidy.

'Of course you can, Mildred,' said Maud cheerily. 'It's on the bed there. Just push up the switch at the side and it makes a hissing sound, then gets warm in a few minutes.'

'Thanks, Maudy,' said Mildred.

She was about to close the door as she left the room when Enid came up behind her.

'I'm just going in to have a chat with Maud,' said Enid. 'Coming?'

'Not yet,' replied Mildred. 'I'm going to have a go at beautifying myself with Maud's magic brush here,' and she skipped off down the corridor back to her room.

'What do you make of our new form-mistress, then?' asked Enid, settling on the end of Maud's bed with her knees pulled up under her chin.

Maud stuffed the last pair of grey-and-black-striped pyjamas into the bottom drawer and closed the wardrobe door.

'She's a bit weird-looking, isn't she?' said Maud. 'I'm surprised H.B. let her over the doorstep. She's so – everything H.B. can't stand, isn't she? Nervous, twittering, doesn't look as if she could control a dead budgerigar – *and* that funny little voice *and* all those frivolous curls!'

Enid laughed. 'Come on,' she said, 'let's go and help Mildred with her hair.'

'Yes, let's,' said Maud, heading for the door. 'I meant to warn her to be careful. It's really easy to get the brush tangled if your hair's long.'

CHAPTER FOUR

Maud and Enid pushed open Mildred's door. 'Be careful with the brush, Mildred,' said Maud. 'It's easy to –'

She stopped abruptly as she saw Mildred sitting on her bed with the styling brush and her hair rolled up in a great messy loop right against her scalp. She was desperately trying to unroll it, but the brush was held as tightly as a fly parcelled up in a spider's web.

'It's got stuck, Maud!' said Mildred, trying not to cry. 'I mean *really* stuck! I've turned it off but it's still burning hot and the brush is black so you can't see where the hair ends and the brush begins.'

'Don't panic, Mildred,' said Enid, trying to sound soothing, despite the horrified tone in her own voice.

'That's right,' said Maud. 'Just leave it and let Enid and me sort it out. Bend your head towards the window so we can see what we're doing.'

Mildred bent her head so that Maud and Enid could assess the situation. It was not good. In the dim light filtering through the narrow castle window, they could see that Mildred had twirled up a large hank of her waist-length hair, which had spiralled round the brush into a hopeless tangle. Maud and Enid exchanged appalled glances. They looked even more horrified when the bell for assembly began to clang urgently through the corridors.

'Oh *no*!' said Mildred, bursting into tears. 'Why on earth do these things always happen to me? I can't go down to assembly like this. H.B. will go bonkers!'

'Hang on, Mildred,' said Maud, jumping up. 'Perhaps I can find someone to help.'

She opened the door just as Ethel Hallow was walking past. Ethel looked in at Mildred. '*Oh* dear,' she said, 'what have you done *now*?'

'Don't be horrible, Ethel,' said Enid. 'This is really bad news. Mildred's got Maud's styling brush stuck in her hair. It'll take all day to untangle. It's *really* serious.'

To everyone's surprise, Ethel looked suddenly genuinely concerned. 'Sorry, Mildred,' she said. 'Of *course* it's awful, but luckily I know *just* what to do. Hang on a sec.'

She went over to the window in an authoritative manner, bent Mildred's head towards her and began busily working on the hair and brush as if she knew exactly how to help. No one could quite see what she was doing and by the time they realized it was too late. Ethel had taken a pair of scissors from the jar on Mildred's window sill and cut the brush out of Mildred's hair, leaving a tuft about three centimetres long and ten centimetres wide.

'Ethel!' exclaimed Maud and Enid together. 'You are *unbelievable*! Look what you've done!'

Mildred leapt up, feeling the space where the brush had been, and rushed to look in the mirror, which hung just below the bats.

'Oh *no*!' she cried. 'I look completely *mad*, Ethel.'

'Well, *you* asked me to help!' said Ethel, sounding offended.

'No, I didn't!' snapped Mildred hotly. 'You just barged in here and hacked a huge lump of my hair off!'

'I thought you'd be pleased,' said Ethel, trying to sound friendly. 'You couldn't have gone to assembly as it was and you'd never have untangled it, not in a million years. Come on, I'll tidy up the rest of it so it doesn't notice so much. I'm really good at hairdressing – I did a course last year. Quick, or we'll *all* be late for assembly.'

CHAPTER FIVE

'What on *earth* have you done to your hair, Mildred Hubble?' exclaimed Miss Hardbroom, as Form Three trooped into the Great Hall for the first-day assembly.

Mildred's hair now resembled a haystack after a night in a force-nine gale. She was very tearful. Ethel had cut the hair roughly, in different lengths, to just below her ears. In some places it was so close to her scalp that there were bald patches showing through.

'I got a styling brush stuck in it, Miss Hardbroom,' sniffed Mildred.

'– and I cut it off for her, Miss Hardbroom,' simpered Ethel. 'She was really upset, so I tried to shape it into a style for her, to neaten it up.'

'Well, let that be a lesson to you, Mildred,' said Miss Hardbroom. 'Trying to do your hair in unsuitably frivolous styles. No good can ever come of all this preening and primping. I'm always warning you girls, but do you ever listen? My goodness, Miss Granite will have her work cut out with you in her class.' She turned away and dismissed the subject of Mildred's hair from her mind.

Mildred, however, couldn't think of anything else. Her long hair had been such a part of her daily routine, plaiting it each morning and brushing it each night. In fact, she hadn't realized quite how upset she would feel at the prospect of presenting herself to the world without it.

'I wish I could turn the clock back,' said Mildred glumly when they had finally been allowed to take their lunch break after two hours of assembly with Miss Cackle droning on about the joys of the Academy and Miss Hardbroom grimly reminding the pupils of the high standards and traditional values expected of one and all. Form Three hastily stuffed down their swede-and-cabbage risotto and rushed out to sit in the yard for half an hour of sunshine before they were trapped with Miss Granite for the rest of the day.

'Don't keep thinking about it, Mildred,' said Maud kindly. 'It won't take long to grow again – well, it'll be *quite* a while, but it'll only be a few weeks before it loses that just-cut look. Perhaps I could try and neaten it up a bit.'

'I'd rather you didn't,' said Mildred hastily. 'I don't want to lose any *more* if you don't mind – thanks all the same.'

'*I* think it looks quite cool, actually,' said Enid, ruffling the top of Mildred's head. 'It's quite fashionable to have that hacked-off look at the moment.'

'Just shut up, Enid, OK?' said Maud, seeing Mildred's shoulders hunch up round her ears. 'Let's try and change the subject, shall we? I wonder what it's going to be like with Miss Granite for the year.'

'*Anything*'ll be better than H.B.,' said Mildred. 'Nothing could be worse than another year of traditional values and always being wrong, however hard you try. Even if she *does* seem a bit weird, Miss Granite looks quite sweet really – what you can see of her. The only bit you can really make out is her nose! Anyway, we'll find out what she's like any minute now. We've got double potions with her when the bell goes.'

When the girls filed into the potion lab at the end of break, Miss Granite was already there, opening all the windows to let some air into the hot and stuffy room. Textbooks were laid out on the desks and everyone settled themselves on to their stools and looked up expectantly at their new teacher.

'Good after*noon*, girls,' said Miss Granite in her squeaky voice, which seemed to have gone up an octave since they had heard her in the playground that morning. 'I'd like you to take it easy this afternoon. You may all look through the *Year Three Spell Sessions Handbook*, find some spells which may be of interest to you and learn them by heart. You can try out a few if you like. Now you're in Year Three *I* don't expect to be telling you what to do all the time.'

The girls felt rather confused. Miss Hardbroom never allowed them to do anything at all without hours of instruction and warnings of dire consequences if they didn't read every paragraph fifteen times.

'Excuse me, Miss Granite,' said

Ethel, putting up her hand. 'Is there any particular spell you might like us to study?'

'Not really,' squeaked Miss Granite vaguely. 'Whatever interests you, dear.' And to Form Three's utter amazement, Miss Granite took out a long bundle of grey knitting from her desk and began to knit in a most intense manner. The girls sat with their mouths open, left completely to their own devices.

'This is really *bizarre*,' whispered Maud to Mildred.

'Perhaps it's always like this in Year Three,' said Enid. 'You know, more *relaxed*.'

'*I* think it's brilliant,' said Mildred, 'just doing stuff on our own. Working at our own pace. Suits me! I'm going to see what I can find in our new Year Three spell book.'

Everyone except Ethel seemed to quite enjoy the new arrangement. Ethel was one of those rare people who thoroughly enjoyed exams and rotas and carrying out detailed instructions which she had grimly studied beforehand. It didn't seem right to be looking up any spell she felt like while the decidedly odd Miss Granite sat knitting at her desk, resembling an overgrown shrub, not teaching them anything at all.

The rest of the girls quickly adapted

to the new laid-back teaching style and leaned on their desks, chatting about the holidays or doodling in their rough notebooks. Enid and Maud were boldly playing a spirited game of noughts and crosses (best of ten) on the cover of Maud's potions exercise book. Only Mildred was actually doing some work. She had found a chapter completely devoted to a spell to generate growth and she immediately began to wonder if she could use it to repair the damage to her hair. It was a very complicated spell, full of unintelligible formulae,

and maths was never Mildred's strong point. She glanced up at Miss Granite, who was half hidden by her hair and turned-up collar and the ever-growing pile of knitting.

'Excuse me, Miss Granite,' said Mildred, putting up her hand. 'Could you help me with this regrowth spell?'

Miss Granite turned her head in Mildred's direction, knitting needles still busily clicking.

'Just look it up in your dictionary of formulae, dear,' she replied. 'You have *got* one, haven't you?'

'Yes,' said Mildred. 'But it's a bit complicated –'

'Well, it's about time you knew how to do things for yourself, dear,' squeaked Miss Granite. 'Now you're in Year Three, I don't want you bothering *me* every five minutes.'

'Sorry, Miss Granite,' muttered Mildred.

'Perhaps *I* can help you, Mildred,' said Ethel, leaning over Mildred's shoulder. 'What's the problem?'

'It's all right, Ethel,' said Mildred guardedly. 'I can work it out by myself, thanks.'

'Oh, go on, Mildred,' wheedled Ethel. 'I'm really good at maths and it's a bit boring with no proper lesson today. I'm sure I could help.'

The most annoying thing about Ethel was her ability to convince you that she might, just this *once*, be truly sorry about whatever unpleasant thing she'd done recently and was actually going to make amends. Mildred fell for it every time.

'*Well*,' she said in an uncertain voice, 'it's this regrowth spell. Look, there are six pages telling you how to make it up. I can get the part about the ingredients – you know, tendrils of Parthenosis and sixteen dewdrops from a spider's web without breaking the strands, that sort of stuff – but I can't understand all these formulae and it won't work unless you can understand the whole thing.'

'Easy-peasy,' smiled Ethel. 'I can do this standing on my head. Is it for your hair?'

Mildred nodded.

'Well, budge up,' said Ethel, smiling happily. 'It's the least I can do after making you look like a scarecrow – though I *was* only trying to help you out of a jam.'

'Thanks, Ethel,' said Mildred. 'It's really good of you.'

'Don't mention it,' smiled Ethel.

CHAPTER SIX

Mildred sat on the edge of her bed, wearing a grey nightie, clutching a test-tube of purple liquid which bubbled and frothed at the top like a fizzy drink. Maud and Enid were huddled behind her, both wearing black-and-grey-striped pyjamas. The first day had finally come to a close and Form Three were supposed to be winding down before lights-out.

Miss Granite had the same relaxed attitude to bedtime as she did to everything else and had told the girls to blow out their own candles by eight thirty, before she wandered off into the school without a backward glance. This gave Mildred a proper opportunity to test the regrowth potion that Ethel had helped her to make.

'What are you supposed to *do* with it?' asked Maud.

'It says you have to apply it,' answered Mildred, 'so I suppose you have to dibble it on to whatever you want to regrow.'

'*I* think you ought to massage it in,' said Enid, 'like shampoo. I'll do it for you, if you like, but I'll need some rubber gloves or I might grow huge great hands!'

'I brought some rubber gloves from the potion lab,' said Mildred. 'I thought we'd probably need some.'

'I'm not sure about this,' said Maud. 'Perhaps we ought to check it with someone first.'

'Like – who?' asked Mildred. 'We can hardly ask H.B., and Miss Granite's in some dream world of her own. Ethel seemed pretty confident about it and it's the right colour. Let's go for it!'

'Hang on,' said Maud, 'I'll get a towel.'

She took a towel from the back of a chair and draped it round Mildred's neck.

Enid pulled on the rubber gloves and, taking the test-tube very carefully from Mildred, poured the contents drop by drop among the roots of Mildred's hair, working it in all over until the potion was completely used up. It fizzed slightly as it touched Mildred's scalp.

'There you go,' said Enid, standing on tiptoe and peering all round the top of Mildred's glistening head. 'Every strand's covered in it.'

'Now what?' said Mildred, sitting stiffly on the bed, too nervous to move.

'I s'pose we just wait,' said Maud. 'Perhaps you have to sleep in it – you know, like nit lotion.'

'Well, nothing seems to be happening yet,' said Mildred. 'Perhaps it isn't going to work anyway. It *did* seem too good to be true.'

'Do you think Miss Granite's *always* going to be like she was today?' asked Maud. 'It really is a bit *strange* that she's turned up in a school like this, don't you think? I can't imagine H.B. approving of her do-it-yourself style of teaching for very long – can you?'

CHAPTER SEVEN

Stalking along the corridor below, Miss Hardbroom was thinking exactly the same thought as Maud. She had craftily called a staff meeting, ostensibly so that they could all discuss how the first day had progressed, but really it was so she could ask Miss Granite a few probing questions without looking as if she was picking on the new teacher. Miss Cackle's Academy had needed a new teacher because the previous one, Miss Gribble, had left after only one term, completely unable to maintain any discipline, and it had been necessary to hire a replacement very quickly. Miss Granite's application form had sounded wonderful, and that marvellous name – Granite, so strong and purposeful. Such a pity that they didn't meet her until the day before school began. Miss Hardbroom hardly knew what to say when this strange, shuffling person arrived, half hidden in the most unruly hair (such a bad example to the girls) and with a voice like a hysterical mouse. But of course Miss Cackle had been kindness itself, as usual, and had insisted they give Miss Granite a chance. Sometimes Miss Cackle was just too feeble for her own good, reflected Miss Hardbroom bitterly.

The meeting was in the small staff room, just below Form Three's row of bedrooms. Miss Hardbroom was the first to arrive and she set about putting glasses of water and pencils and paper by each chair. There seemed to be quite a lot of noise coming from above. In fact, it sounded as if *girls were running about* in the corridors up there! Miss Hardbroom was just about to set off and investigate when Miss Cackle pushed open the door and came in, followed by Miss Bat, so she decided to wait until after the meeting.

Up in Mildred's room, Enid, Mildred and Maud were perched in a row on the edge of the bed, feeling a bit let down after their initial excitement about the potion.

'It's not going to work, is it?' sighed Mildred. 'Let's face it, I'm just stuck looking barmy for the next six months. Why don't we go to bed now, before someone comes up to investigate all the messing about in the corridor and we all get into trouble.'

'Good thinking, Mildred,' said Maud. 'Everyone's being really silly out there tonight. At least we're the goody-goodies for once!'

The whole day had seemed really topsy-turvy, reflected Mildred, as she snuggled down under the bedclothes, with Tabby happily settled on her chest, kneading the covers and purring loudly. To her surprise, she found herself feeling a bit uneasy about the happy-go-lucky attitude of Miss Granite as she listened to the general mayhem going on outside her door. Someone had set up some skittles at one end of the corridor and several girls were having a bowling contest, punctuated with loud cheering. H.B. was right really. It only took five minutes of slipping standards and everyone seemed to have forgotten how to behave.

Mildred put a hand up to her hair. It had dried into a crispy bird's-nest and obviously wasn't going to do anything, so she blew out her candle and attempted to fall asleep, despite the escalating noise outside. 'Oh well,' she thought contentedly, 'at least *I* won't be in the firing line when H.B. suddenly blows a fuse at them all.'

A few minutes later, as Mildred was just drifting off, Tabby started patting her neck.

'Stop it, Tab,' said Mildred, batting him off in the dark. At once, Tabby bounced back on to the bed and started pouncing on Mildred's head and shoulders, making darting pats, rather as he had done when he was a kitten trying to catch a string pulled along the floor. '*Tabby!*' exclaimed Mildred crossly. 'What's got into you? Stop it! Get off me!'

CHAPTER EIGHT

ownstairs, in the staff room, all the teachers had arrived and were seated round the table. The shouts and bumping in the corridor above were very noticeable and Miss Hardbroom, knowing that it was coming from Form Three's bedroom corridor, realized that this would be an excellent way to challenge Miss Granite's methods of teaching and control without looking as if she was being too hasty or interfering. Miss Cackle assisted matters by commenting on the noise.

'What *is* going on up there, Miss Hardbroom?' she asked, raising her eyes to the ceiling. 'It sounds as if the girls are having a party. I *know* there are always high spirits on the first day back, but it really is getting rather late and I can hardly hear myself *think*!'

Miss Hardbroom stood up and turned her steely gaze in the direction of Miss Granite, who sat hunched in her seat at the far end of the table, half hidden by her cape collar and bush-like hair.

'Miss Granite,' said Miss Hardbroom, 'the corridor upstairs is inhabited by Form Three – your girls, are they not? Perhaps you are not aware of the *stringent* rules concerning bedtimes at Miss Cackle's Academy? Candles out for *all* pupils, even the fifth-years, by eight thirty at the very latest. I must point out –'

She stopped in mid-flow. Everyone

could suddenly hear a very loud and desperate miaowing coming from directly outside the window, with frantic screams wafting down from somewhere above. Miss Drill leapt up and rushed to peer out into the twilight.

'I think you'd all better come and take a look at this,' she said.

Outside the window they saw Mildred's cat, Tabby, hanging on desperately to a great mass of dark stuff, which was descending in a steady, fluid motion towards the courtyard thirty metres below.

Upstairs, Mildred's screams had alerted the pupils in the corridor. Maud and Enid were first on the scene. By the light of the corridor-lanterns, they could all see that the potion had worked – rather too well, unfortunately. No one had paused to think how you could stop the hair if it started growing, and there it was, twisting and tumbling all around the room, with Mildred jumping up and down on the bed, trying to fight her way clear so that she could breathe.

'Maud!' she screamed. 'Tabby's gone out of the window! He was trying to catch the hair when it started growing after I'd gone to sleep – I didn't realize what he was doing and pushed him off and now he's gone out with the hair! Oh, Maud! Can't you do something? Please!'

For a few moments, nobody knew what to do, as the hair was growing in

a terrifyingly unstoppable way. Some of it was coiling up under the bed, more was cascading out of the window and the rest poured out through the open door into the corridor, twirling around people's ankles like a speeded-up film of ivy invading a ruin.

Maud and Enid snapped out of their trance and sprang into action.

'Come out into the corridor, Mildred,' shrieked Enid. 'Move away from the hair – start trying to drag it behind you.'

Mildred climbed off the bed and made for the door, while Maud burrowed through the hair towards the window so she could start trying to haul in the huge hank that was plummeting out into space.

'Hang on, Tab,' yelled Maud. 'Nearly got you!'

'*Have* you, Maud?' shouted Mildred over her shoulders. '*Have* you got him?'

'Yes!' lied Maud, who could see Tabby six metres below, yowling his head off outside the lit window beneath. 'Just keep going down the corridor, Millie – don't look back!'

Maud pulled at the hair with all her might, like a fisherman hauling in a net, trying not to jerk it so that Tabby could hold on better, but Mildred's hair was very silky and kept slipping through her fingers.

The room was full of girls desperately trying to hold the hair

back from Mildred's neck and
shoulders as she fled down the
corridor, the hair flowing like a train
behind her. Meanwhile, Enid and
Maud hung out of the window,
clutching at handfuls of hair and
shouting words of encouragement to
Tabby, who was now moaning in a
deep, unearthly way that echoed eerily
around the whole school. The poor

first-years huddled in their beds, already tearful with second thoughts about the school they now found themselves in, listened with horror to the sinister noise of what sounded like a distant ghost-cat and trembled with fear and longing to be at home again.

Mildred reached the end of the corridor, surrounded by a large crowd of pupils, all trying to help by tossing the hair behind her and trying to stop it snaking through the open bedroom doors as she passed by. She stopped for a moment to catch her breath.

'Is Tabby all right?' she called anxiously, attempting to look back. 'Has anyone got a copy of *Year Three Spell Sessions*?'

They all stopped in their tracks as Miss Hardbroom materialized at the top of the stairs.

CHAPTER NINE

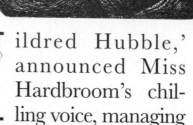

'Mildred Hubble,' announced Miss Hardbroom's chilling voice, managing to sound quiveringly irate and slightly weary at the same time. 'Mildred *Hubble*. What on earth have you been doing up here, inciting the entire form into some sort of riot?'

'It's – it's my hair, Miss Hardbroom,' wittered Mildred. 'Something terrible has happened to my hair.'

'I can see that,' said Miss Hardbroom. She paused for a

moment, then continued with a sneery smile. 'I took one look at the situation and thought to myself, "Mildred Hubble seems to be having what you girls might term a bad-hair day."'

This was such an unexpected witticism from Miss Hardbroom that several of the girls burst out laughing. Now that Mildred had stopped, the hair was bunching up over the top of her head like an out-of-control candyfloss machine and attempting to loop over her face on to the floor.

'Oh, for goodness' sake!' exclaimed Miss Hardbroom. She muttered the words of the reversal spell and directed her fingers in a zap at the hair, which suddenly stopped growing.

Just at that moment, Ethel's door opened and she came out.

'I was trying to sleep, Miss Hardbroom,' she said, rubbing her eyes as if she had just woken up. 'Is there anything I can do to help?'

'Yes, you can, Ethel,' said Miss Hardbroom. 'Go and fetch a pair of scissors so that I can restore some orderly calm to us all.'

'Is Tabby back in yet?' said Mildred. 'I don't want to cut my hair so that he falls off the end.'

'Don't worry, Mildred,' called Maud, shouldering her way through the carpet of hair. 'We've got him. Look, he's perfectly all right.'

Tabby didn't look perfectly all right at all. He was wild-eyed and frozen with terror, riveted on to the front of Maud's pyjamas, emitting a strange pulsing sound like a deep growl crossed with the continuous whine of a faulty vacuum cleaner.

'What length do you want this, Mildred Hubble?' asked Miss Hardbroom, snapping the scissors impatiently.

'Just like it was before, please, Miss Hardbroom,' replied Mildred meekly.

Ethel came running up with the scissors and Miss Hardbroom cut the hair (rather jaggedly) so that it was back to its usual length.

'Would you like me to do the spell to clear the remainder of the hair away, Miss Hardbroom?' asked Ethel. 'I've studied this spell and I know all about it. I could have stopped the hair growing if Mildred had asked, but it didn't *occur* to me that she would actually attempt to *use* such an advanced spell – *and* for such a trivial reason – *and* at this time of night!'

'It's all right, thank you, Ethel,' said Miss Hardbroom approvingly. 'I'll deal with it. Now back to bed with all of you. Not another peep out of anyone. I'll have to have *another* word with Miss Granite about you, Mildred. She obviously has no idea how to deal with you. I might have known who it was at the bottom of the hoo-ha going on above us in the staff room tonight.'

As the girls picked their way back through the swathes of hair to their rooms, Miss Hardbroom chanted the final part of the spell and the remaining hair evaporated into thin air. Mildred put a hand up to her regrown hair to make sure it was still there and, to her relief, it was.

'Thanks for nothing, Ethel,' muttered Mildred, as she passed Ethel's door. 'You always manage to drop me in it, don't you?'

Ethel smiled jauntily. 'Keep your hair on, Mildred,' she said, as she closed the door with a triumphant flourish.

CHAPTER TEN

Mildred was utterly exhausted when she woke the next morning after the horror of the Bad-hair Day. Tabby was still in a terrible state. He seemed to have gone into a trance, hanging on to Mildred's pillow with a wide-eyed, almost vacant stare, as if he could see dreadful things in the distance. It had taken Mildred half an hour to prise him from Maud's front the night before, leaving a large rip in Maud's pyjamas where he wouldn't let go. Now he leapt on to Mildred's shoulders and clung tightly with his claws as she struggled to plait her regrown hair and put on her uniform.

Maud put her head round the door with her own cat, Midnight (a nice, normal, easygoing black one), perched like a parrot on her shoulder.

'How are you feeling, Mildred?' Maud asked kindly.

'Neck's a bit stiff,' replied Mildred, 'and Tabby seems to have had a complete nervous breakdown, but apart from that everything's fine.' She smiled ruefully.

'Miss Granite just came round and said we're all to take our brooms down to the courtyard for some cat and broomstick practice,' said Maud.

'Oh *no!*' said Mildred. 'Not yet. Not straight away. Look at Tab. He just won't be able to cope. Do you think we could leave our cats in the bedroom?'

'No chance,' said Maud. '"Year Threes must fly with their cats at all times"! Don't you remember? It's traditional. From this year on, the cats have to come with us everywhere.'

'You haven't got any travel-sickness pills or anything, have you, Maud?' asked Mildred hopefully. 'Perhaps he'd feel a bit calmer if he had one of those. He really looks as if he's lost his marbles.'

'Sorry, Mil,' said Maud. 'I've only got some vitamin pills and I don't think they'd be any use – although they *are* supposed to make children more intelligent if they take them regularly. Perhaps they might work on cats!'

'Don't be mean, Maud,' said Mildred with a smile. 'He's not *that* dim!'

After breakfast, Form Three trooped off to the schoolyard, Mildred with Tabby clinging to her front like a koala, where Miss Granite was waiting for them. She was sitting on a bench, rummaging in her large bag, while the girls stood around holding their brooms and cats, wondering what to do. Miss Granite pulled out an apple and began to eat it noisily, her dark glasses twinkling in the sun, smiling at everyone.

'Excuse me, Miss Granite,' said Ethel, stepping forward, her broomstick hovering alongside with her cat, Nightstar, neatly perched on the back. 'Is there any particular manoeuvre you would like us to practise? I'm especially good at nosedives and speed loop-the-loops. Would you like me to –'

'Whatever you want, dear,' said Miss Granite in her strange, high-pitched squeak. 'I'm feeling a little tired today and I think I might go and lie down. Perhaps you would like to take the lesson for me – er – what is your name, dear?'

'Ethel Hallow, Miss Granite,' said Ethel, almost purring with deep happiness at the thought of having Form Three in her clutches.

'Ethel,' said Miss Granite, 'you make sure everyone does the right stuff. I'll come along later and check.'

Mildred glanced at Maud as Miss Granite waddled up the steps into the school.

'This is *so* strange,' said Mildred. 'She doesn't seem to know what to do with us, does she?'

'*She* doesn't,' said Ethel, 'but *I* do. Come along now, Form Three, *I'm* in charge. Would you please remove that joke of a witch's cat from your clothing, Mildred Hubble, and apply it to the back of your broomstick.'

'Why don't you lay off, Ethel Hallow?' said Enid. '*You*'re not the teacher, whatever our "hey-man" new form-mistress says. I'm beginning to wish we'd still got H.B. if we're going to have to put up with you bossing us all around.'

'It's true, Ethel,' said Maud. 'We're all perfectly capable of organizing our own flying lesson if Miss Granite's left us to it. We don't need any helpful comments from you.'

'Tabs has had a dreadful shock, Ethel,' said Mildred, putting her arms protectively round Tabby and smoothing his head. 'He nearly died last night, dangling out of the window like that. He's stressed, poor thing. I'm really glad we've got an easy day and I'm certainly not going to force him to do any flying.'

But Ethel had other ideas. She hoisted herself calmly on to her broomstick, Nightstar bolt upright on the back, and swooped past Mildred, snatching Tabby from her arms with one expert grab.

'Nonsense, Mildred,' Ethel yelled, as she zoomed upwards towards the roof turrets. '*Stress* indeed! What this cat needs is to *pull himself together*! He's been flying for two years now. He knows how to do it. Look at him!'

Mildred looked. Tabby was half on the back of the broom and half hanging on to Ethel's sash. He was so shocked that he wasn't making a sound. To make matters worse, Nightstar, who was extremely territorial about his broomstick (and Ethel), was taking vicious swipes at Tabby's ears every time Ethel turned her back.

'Ethel!' shrieked Mildred. 'Bring him back! He'll fall off. *Please!*'

'Come back, Ethel,' shouted Maud, as Ethel and the two cats disappeared from view into a swirl of mist surrounding the topmost turrets.

A few members of Form Three thought Ethel was right and that Tabby would be safe with her giving him a special lesson, but most of the girls were firmly on Mildred's side, patting her shoulder and calling up to the rooftops for Ethel to come back at once.

'It's no use,' said Mildred. 'I'll have to go and get him back. Oh, *Maud*. I'm just a walking disaster area at the moment – well, *all the time*, really – aren't I? It's just been one thing after another. I'll *never* keep up with Ethel; she'll be doing loop-the-loops and goodness knows what.'

'Don't worry, Mil,' said Enid. 'We'll come up with you, won't we, Maud?'

'You bet!' said Maud. 'With three of us we can head her off and perhaps make her see reason.'

They all snorted with grim laughter at this unlikely prospect.

'Come on, then!' called Mildred, as she set off in hot pursuit. 'We'd better be quick.'

CHAPTER ELEVEN

There was no sign of Ethel among the rooftops and turrets as the three friends landed on a wide patch of slanting roof. They propped their brooms next to them and kept quiet in case they could hear the sound of Ethel flying. Surprisingly, there's quite a lot of noise from someone on a broomstick, especially if they are moving fast. The broomstick itself makes a swishing noise as it cuts through the air, and gymslips and cloaks tend to flap in the wind. But although they kept completely still, there was no sound from anywhere.

'Let's split up,' suggested Enid. 'I'll take the lower courtyard at the back.'

'I'll go over the wall above the forest,' said Maud. 'You can see for miles down the mountain if you just go a little way.'

'OK,' said Mildred. 'I'll stay up here for a minute. She might be hiding somewhere and if she hears you both fly off she might think it's safe to come out.'

'Good thinking, Batgirl,' said Enid.

'Good luck!' said Maud.

Mildred leaned back against the slates as Maud and Enid took off from the ridge tiles, their cats looking calm and confident on the back of their brooms. Mildred felt the usual guilty twinge as she imagined, for a brief second, how different it might have been if she had been given a sensible black cat all those years ago. Just as quickly, she pushed the disloyal thought out of her mind and craned forward as she heard the unmistakable sound of someone taking off from the other side of the roof. Mildred's theory had been spot on.

Ethel passed above her head by several centimetres, close enough for Mildred to see Tabby, now hanging upside down like a sloth, with Nightstar swiping at Tabby's paws where they curled round the top of the broom. Tabby let out a desperate yowl when he saw his mistress below him, and Mildred, completely forgetting where she was, made a lunge upwards with both hands to pull him off. She missed, and three awful things happened at the same time. First of all,

Mildred lost her balance and began sliding down the tiles, scrabbling madly with her fingers as she slithered towards the edge. Secondly, Tabby, who thought Mildred was reaching up to save him, let go of the broom and tumbled off, bouncing and yowling as he tried to save himself on the other side of the roof, and thirdly, Mildred dislodged her precious new broom, which plummeted to the yard far below, before she had time to command it.

Ethel heard the commotion as Mildred began to fall and turned in mid-air, putting the broom into a superb nosedive and coming up underneath Mildred at the very moment that she shot off the roof into space. Mildred fell perfectly into place behind Ethel, grabbing her round her waist and nearly squashing the indignant Nightstar. The cat's sense of

balance was so amazing that he merely
jumped neatly out of the way and
settled straight back into his usual
upright stance, looking faintly annoyed.

'Yessss!' exclaimed Ethel. 'Say thank you, Mildred! I just saved your life.'

'Wait, Ethel!' yelled Mildred, as Ethel aimed for the courtyard where Form Three were gazing anxiously upwards.

'We must go back and find Tabby. He's still up there by himself. He might be hurt.'

'Not me!' said Ethel. 'I've had enough of trying to help you and that stupid animal. He's a *cat*, Mildred – even if he *has* only got one brain cell *and* he's not a *real* witch's cat. Even a farmyard tabby knows how to fall and has the usual nine lives. He'll find his own way down.'

Ethel landed gracefully amid the excited pupils, and Mildred jumped off as quickly as possible, embarrassed to be seen hanging on to her arch enemy.

'Pity about your new broom,' said Ethel. 'Now it's just like your old one.

Poor you. Flying really isn't your strong point, is it?'

Mildred saw that her broom had hit the corrugated-iron roof of the broomshed as it fell and had completely broken in half. At this point Enid and Maud arrived back in the yard and found Mildred holding her ruined broom, trying not to cry.

'What's happened?' asked Enid, putting an arm round Mildred.

'*Everything*,' said Mildred, bursting into tears. 'This term can't get any worse, can it? Now Tabby's up on the rooftops somewhere, probably unconscious, and my lovely new broom's in exactly the same state as the old one. If only Miss Granite would take *charge* a bit, these awful things wouldn't keep happening.'

'I'll go and fetch some tape, Millie,' said Maud. 'Strong sticky tape will fix anything and I think I've got some really good glue somewhere.'

Maud returned with a roll of tape and a tube of superglue. They spread the glue around the splintered spikes of wood and jammed them together, then bound the join with several layers of tape.

'Better leave it for a few hours so it can set,' said Enid.

'But I can't leave Tabby up there,' said Mildred. 'He might be hurt. Can I borrow your broom, Maud, *please*? I *promise* nothing will happen to it – I'll be *so* careful,' she added, as she saw Maud glancing doubtfully at the bundle of sticky tape. 'I'll just take a quick look around and come straight back if I can't see him. *Please*, Maudy.'

'All right,' said Maud, trying not to sound nervous. 'But only be ten minutes, OK?'

CHAPTER TWELVE

Mildred jumped on to Maud's broom and was up among the turrets within seconds. She landed on a flat area with an old chimney stack in the middle and dismounted so that she could take a calm look around. To her delight, she saw Tabby at once. He was two rooftops away, curled up in a miserable hunch underneath a window.

'Tabby!' called Mildred. 'Don't move! I'm coming over.'

Tabby didn't respond at all. He was making his low, growly whining noise, looking across at Mildred with eyes like saucers.

Suddenly Mildred heard a voice coming from the window – an unmistakable high-pitched, squeaky voice. 'Who is out there?' called the voice. 'Come along now, I know someone's there!'

Mildred ducked behind the chimney stack as Miss Granite leaned out of the window and spotted Tabby cowering just below the window sill. She reached out, bundled him up the

wall into her arms and disappeared back inside the room. Mildred flew down to the courtyard.

'Well?' called Maud, as her friend came in to land. 'Any luck?'

'*Sort* of,' said Mildred glumly. 'Miss Granite's room is up there and Tabs was outside her window, so she's taken him into her room. At least he'll be safe inside and he didn't look as though he'd broken anything. He did look a bit *barmy* though. If anything else happens to him, I don't think he'll *ever* get back to normal.'

'Are you going to ask Miss Granite if you can collect him?' asked Enid.

'Tricky,' said Mildred. 'We're not supposed to go up that high. On the other hand, Miss Granite doesn't seem to mind *what* we do.'

'Doesn't she?' said a squeaky voice, as Miss Granite materialized, H.B.-style, behind them. 'I think you'll find that I *do* mind what's going on behind my back. Now then – Mildred Hubble, isn't it? I'd like to know what your cat was doing fifty metres up in an area that's out of bounds to you girls.'

'I – um – er –' mumbled Mildred wretchedly. 'I was – um – er – I took a wrong turning and got a bit lost and – um – Tabby sort of fell off. He's still feeling a bit delicate after the – you know – *incident* last night with the hair-growing spell.'

'Oh yes, *that*,' squeaked Miss Granite. She took a step closer to Mildred and, for some reason, Mildred felt a sudden chill. Perhaps it was the tinted glasses, which had a sort of blank look and seemed a little sinister. 'I hope you weren't *snooping*, Mildred Hubble. I hope you weren't *spying* on me.'

'Oh *no*, Miss Granite,' said Mildred.

'Not at all! It was just an accident that I was up there.'

'You seem to have rather a lot of accidents, Mildred Hubble,' said Miss Granite. 'In fact, as far as *I* have seen, you've had some sort of accident every five minutes since term began, and from what I have *heard*, it's been exactly the same for the entire two years you've been here. Anyway, just keep away from my room,' she continued, 'or you'll be sorry. Understand?'

'Yes, Miss Granite,' mumbled Mildred, blushing. 'But could I go and collect Tabby first?'

'What did I just *say*, girl?' exploded Miss Granite, sounding like an irate hamster. 'Your *ridiculous* cat is perfectly safe where he is. *I'll* bring him to you when *I* see fit. Until then, the subject is closed. Now then, girls –' she turned to the rest of the class, who had gradually reassembled in the yard – 'it's time for your lunch, followed by an afternoon of chanting with Miss Bat. Good morning.'

She disappeared just as the lunch bell clanged out across the yard.

'Wow!' said Enid. 'What a change.'

'That was really *weird*,' said Mildred. 'She's still got that funny voice, but she sounded really terrifying – almost like H.B. What did you think, Maud?'

'Perhaps she wakes up in a bad

temper,' said Maud. 'She did say she was going to have a rest, didn't she?'

'Well,' said Mildred, 'at least Tabs is OK. She'll probably give him to me later. Come on, let's go and see what horrors await us at lunch. Someone said it was spinach with fried eggs on it today.'

'Per-*lease!*' laughed Maud.

CHAPTER THIRTEEN

Evening arrived and Miss Granite did not bring Tabby down from her room. Mildred tried to pluck up courage to ask if it would be possible to fetch him, but Miss Granite seemed very grumpy and unapproachable, and somehow Mildred could sense that she would go berserk if anyone suggested it.

Everyone was sent to bed early that night. Miss Granite announced that she wanted them all asleep by eight thirty after their disgraceful behaviour the previous night. Miss Hardbroom materialized next to Miss Granite as she was in mid-rant at the girls, who were lined up nervously in the Form Three bedroom corridor.

'I'm pleased to see that you are taking a firm line with these girls, Miss Granite,' said Miss Hardbroom approvingly. 'They really do need to be kept in order at all times. Give them an inch and they'll take a mile, as we saw yesterday – especially with Mildred Hubble in the class.'

'I *quite* agree, Miss Hardbroom.' Miss Granite nodded. 'We've all decided to pull together, girls, haven't we? No more nonsense. From now on it's hard work and discipline all the way.'

A while later, when everyone was supposed to be safely in their beds, Mildred crept from her room and knocked at Maud's door.

'Can I come in, Maud?' she

whispered. 'Just for a sec.'

'Do be careful, Mil,' said Maud, opening the door just wide enough to let Mildred sneak inside. 'Miss Granite seems to have had a personality transplant. All that easygoing stuff and now she's turned into Attila the Hun!'

'There's something *funny* going on, Maud,' said Mildred. 'I don't know what it is, but there's something *creepy* about her. Her voice is so odd – I mean, I've met people with high voices before, but hers doesn't sound real. And the way she isn't giving us any lessons – it's as if she doesn't know how to teach. Maybe she isn't a real teacher at all. Maybe she's an impostor!'

'Well, there's nothing *we* can do about it,' said Maud. 'We'd better just keep out of her way and hope for the best.'

'I'm worried about Tab,' said Mildred. 'Why hasn't she given him back to me? Maybe she's going to use his whiskers for some spell or other. I think I might sneak up and see if I can get him out.'

'*Don't!*' said Maud flatly. 'Just *don't*. I'm sure he'll be OK for one night. She's probably just forgotten. Promise me, Mil – promise you won't do anything silly.'

'Oh, all right,' said Mildred. 'I promise. ''Night, Maud.'

Mildred climbed into bed and pulled the covers up to her chin. The bats were all out on their nightly hunt and the room was silent and lonely without Tabby purring and kneading the covers on her chest. She couldn't bear to lie there knowing her beloved pet might be longing to hear her voice, so she decided to risk disaster. Mildred crept into the corridor and set off up the three spiral staircases which led to the maze of corridors where the teachers had their rooms. As she paused at the foot of the second staircase, she heard someone coming downstairs and ducked behind a display cabinet with a large vase of dried flowers on top of it. It was Miss Hardbroom, wearing outdoor clothes and carrying her broom, with Morgana, her beautiful cat, skittering behind her, trying to keep up. Miss Hardbroom was off to visit her friend Miss Pentangle, who was headmistress of Pentangle's Academy, a neigh-bouring witches' school several mountaintops away. She was pleased that the irritating Miss Granite had

turned over a new leaf and that the
school was quiet and orderly for the
night, just as it should be. She was also
looking forward to an evening of
interesting conversation, as well as a
taxing game of chess and, possibly, just

one glass of sherry, as she was in such a
good mood. Mildred flattened herself
against the wall and held her breath
until she heard the heavy front door
close several floors below with a
resounding thud.

All the rooms had neat brass name-card holders, with the teachers' names inscribed in Gothic lettering, so it only took Mildred a few moments of silent slinking along the top corridor and peering at the name-cards before she found Miss Granite's room. Mildred pressed her ear against the door – it was completely silent from the other side. She called, very softly, 'Tabby! Tabs, it's me.' A loud miaow sounded immediately from the other side of the door. Mildred turned the handle and went in. Tabby was on the far side of the room in a cat-basket on the table.

Mildred was so pleased to see him that she was halfway across the room before she realized that the miaow had come from immediately behind the door. She turned to look back, just as the door swung shut, and nearly jumped out of her skin when she saw Miss Cackle standing behind her.

'Oh, Miss Cackle!' exclaimed Mildred. 'It's you! I'm sorry, I've just come to collect Tabby. I thought perhaps Miss Granite had forgotten.'

'No, Mildred,' said Miss Cackle, smiling kindly, as she always did. 'Miss Granite knew that you would come back and collect Tabby – that's why she decided to hold on to him for a little while longer.'

'I don't know what you mean, Miss Cackle,' said Mildred. 'Why would Miss Granite want to keep Tabby? He wouldn't be any use to her – I don't understand.'

'Let me show you something, my dear,' said Miss Cackle. She took Mildred's arm and led her to a door which opened into a linen cupboard full of towels and sheets. Then, without any warning, she shoved Mildred inside, slammed the door and locked her in.

CHAPTER FOURTEEN

'Miss Cackle!' yelled Mildred. '*Please* let me out. I really don't like the dark.'

'It's all right, Mildred,' said Miss Cackle soothingly. 'It won't be for long. You didn't guess, did you? Let me give you a little clue.' There was a loud cackle of laughter and the voice suddenly changed into Miss Granite's odd squeak. 'Don't you remember what happened last time we met in the middle of the wood, Mildred Hubble, when you turned us all into snails?

Yes, Mildred, Miss Granite is none other than Agatha Cackle, your precious Miss Cackle's twin sister – in a curly wig and hiding behind purple dark glasses. I can't believe that none of you twigged!' Her voice changed back to normal, sounding very like Miss Cackle. 'I must say it's wonderful not to have to put on that awful voice any more. Anyway, my dear, this time the plan's a dead cert and tonight's the night. The only person I was worried about was you, with your knack of always turning up at the wrong time, so with you in the cupboard my plan can't fail. All I have to do is wait till everyone's asleep in their beds. Then, at two o'clock precisely, the other members of my coven arrive at the entrance in the backyard and – hey presto! Abracadabra! – I just saunter down and let them all in and, quick as a flash, the school is mine. Miss

Agatha Cackle's Academy of *Real* Witchcraft. No more of this namby-pamby, play-it-by-the-rules, goody-two-shoes stuff! Now then, what can we turn them all into? It was going to be frogs last time, but you gave me an idea when you turned us into snails; they don't move so fast – much easier to catch. There you are, Mildred. Just occasionally you *do* have an excellent idea. I can't tell you what fun it's been planning all this right under my dear sister's nose – *and* that awful Hardbroom person! They both think they're *so* clever, but they didn't suspect anything. Well, my dear, just make yourself comfy in there. It's going to be a long night!'

She let out a horrible cackling laugh and Mildred could hear her move away from the door.

Mildred took some deep breaths and tried very hard to calm down. She really was afraid of the dark (a great embarrassment for a trainee witch) and this was one of her worst nightmares – being trapped somewhere in the pitch-dark with an enemy outside the door. Half an hour passed by, during which time Mildred could hear Agatha muttering to herself and moving about. She racked her brains as she tried desperately to think of a way out. The shelves in the cupboard were set

back a little way from the door and, as she perched on the edge of some towels, Mildred saw that there was a crack beneath the door where she could see a strip of light from the lantern and Agatha's shadow moving around the room. Mildred realized, with horror, that she must think fast, as she would probably be the first snail! It suddenly dawned on her that if she could change herself into something small, she could sneak out under the door and seek help.

Mildred was becoming something of an expert on the subject of transformation. In her first term she had changed Ethel into a pig by mistake. Next, Ethel had turned Mildred into a frog, and later on Mildred's friend Enid had changed her own cat into a monkey. Mildred's holiday project had been insect spells and she knew how to change herself into either an ant or a caterpillar. To tell you the truth, she wasn't very keen on the idea of turning into either, but in the end she decided that an ant was the best idea. A caterpillar had all those legs to coordinate, plus it was slower and more noticeable. Also, if it was just at the stage where it was going to turn into a chrysalis (and, knowing Mildred's luck, it would be!), the whole thing could get extremely complicated. She didn't fancy the idea of being wrapped up immobile for several weeks, then turning into a butterfly, and by that time she'd have forgotten who she was and what she was supposed to be doing. An ant seemed the better choice. Mildred considered the Witch's Code: 'Spells are never to be used for trivial or selfish reasons.' This was neither. The school, and everyone in it, was in immediate danger. She had never actually turned herself into anything before – although she and Maud had disappeared once when they were trying to make a laughter potion. That had been strange enough, being able to see right through yourself to the chair you were sitting on, but actually turning into something hundreds of times smaller than yourself was quite an unnerving thought. According to the Witch's Code, if you transformed yourself into an animal, you could still change yourself back into a human again. However, this was not the case if someone else changed *you*. In that case you were trapped until the other person removed the spell. Mildred could see that there was really no choice. It was either a snail forever or a temporary ant. She chose the ant.

Mildred braced herself and muttered the words of the spell, wrapping her arms round herself and flexing her fingers into little zaps of energy. It worked. First of all she had a peculiar tingling feeling all over, with a sensation of being pulled inwards very fast from all parts of her body – even her hair. Then, very suddenly, she was an ant – a whole centimetre lower than the base of the door. The transformation was not exactly pleasant, although it didn't hurt and was so fast that she barely had time to panic.

Mildred found that being an ant was very different to the way she had felt when Ethel had turned her into a frog. On that occasion she had still felt very much like herself, despite being hunched into a frog position and being able to jump like an Olympic athlete, but being an ant, she found herself fizzing with manic energy and the compulsion to start zooming about in a sort of frenzy. In fact, it was quite difficult to remember what she was supposed to be doing, as she set off like a rocket into the room. She

narrowly avoided being trodden on by Agatha and scuttled under the bedroom door and out into the corridor. The best thing to have done would have been for Mildred to change herself back once she was safely out of Miss Granite's bedroom, but she found it difficult to focus her ant brain on the intricacies of the reversal spell, especially as she had stumbled across a large cake crumb just outside the door and immediately felt an overwhelming desire to start dragging it back underneath the door towards the airing cupboard.

'What on earth am I doing?' thought Mildred wildly, pushing the crumb away. 'I must get back to Maud and find help.'

She beetled to the top of the stairs as fast as she could, desperately trying to stay focused on getting down the huge stone steps of the spiral staircases and back to the Form Three corridor. Her progress was unfortunately hindered by a trail of cake crumbs, some of them with microscopic smears of jam, and each time she came across

one, Mildred experienced the same all-consuming need to start either eating the crumb (especially those with jam on) or tidying the crumbs back towards Miss Granite's room.

'*Must* get to Maud!' said the ant-Mildred, clambering resolutely over a boulder-sized morsel. 'Must get to Maud. Must get to Maud.'

It seemed to be taking forever, what with her tiny size and the delicious array of crumbs. Each step on all three spiral staircases was as high as a mountain to an ant, even though it was quite fun to find that she could run down the upright part with complete ease. It was just taking *such* a long time.

CHAPTER FIFTEEN

Mildred finally arrived at Maud's door and skimmed underneath with a sigh of relief. At least there were no crumbs of any sort to distract her in Form Three's bedroom corridor, as the pupils were never allowed any sweets or cakes in addition to their three daily meals. If Mildred hadn't been so frantic in her mission to alert Maud, she would have been quite annoyed about the amount of cake crumbs she had encountered in the teachers' wing of the school!

Now she realized that she faced a big problem. How on earth was she going to wake Maud up? Maud was a very heavy sleeper and was actually snoring, which meant she was deeply unconscious. She had a wonderfully calm, straightforward nature and tended to fall asleep the moment her head hit the pillow (unlike Mildred, who was always worried about something she had, or hadn't, done).

By a useful stroke of luck, there was an almost-full moon lighting the room well enough for Mildred to see where everything was, so she zoomed up the bed leg and on to Maud's pillow. The snoring was actually creating a hurricane-force wind as Mildred flicked her antennae against Maud's chin.

Maud obviously felt the antennae in her sleep, because she raised her hand to brush the ant-Mildred away. Fortunately, Mildred had proper ant-

like reactions and zipped to one side before Maud's hand touched her chin.

'This is hopeless,' thought Mildred. 'Even if I *do* wake her up and she sees me, she'll just think I'm an ant.' She rested on her middle legs and absent-mindedly combed her antennae with her front ones while she tried to work out how she could let Maud know that she was Mildred and not an ant.

The same situation had occurred when Mildred had been turned into a frog by Ethel, but Tabby had recognized the frog-Mildred and cuddled up to her so that Maud had begun to wonder about things, especially as Mildred had gone missing. This time, Maud had no idea that Mildred was anywhere except in her own comfy bed next door. Mildred ran down the bedspread on to the floor and decided to skim up the leg of the small homework table under the window. By the light of the moon, Mildred could see that Maud had been in the middle of writing a letter. The pupils all had to write home once a week, telling their families what a happy and studious time they were having at Miss Cackle's. Miss Hardbroom always read through the letters before she took them to the post, so it was difficult to write anything other than 'I am very happy. The food is wonderful and I am doing lots of homework.' Maud hadn't got much further than, 'Dear all, I am so glad to be back with my friends.' The rest of the page glowed blue-white in the moonlight, next to the bottle of black ink, which was uncovered as Maud had forgotten to put the top back on.

'It really *is* more like a prison than a school,' reflected Mildred glumly. 'Perhaps I ought to just stay as an ant and live upstairs eating all the crumbs from the teachers' cakes for the rest of my life.'

CHAPTER SIXTEEN

Back in Miss Granite's room, Agatha still had quite a lot of work to do before two o'clock. She had put Tabby's cat-basket on to a chair and assembled a neat pile of shoeboxes and jam jars on the table. The boxes were all labelled Form One, Form Two and so on, and the jam jars were individually marked with the teachers' names in indelible black pen. Agatha sat at the table, busily cutting out circles of paper with air-holes punched in them to go on the jars. She had already jabbed holes in the lids of the boxes and had a big bag of leaves and grass on the floor ready to go into everything so that the snails would be comfortable while Agatha and her coven decided what to do with them. The military precision of the operation was chilling to watch.

By twelve thirty everything was ready and Agatha settled down with a large mug of tea and a packet of biscuits before the expected invasion at two o'clock sharp.

Down in Maud's room, Mildred had devised a plan of action which could only have been dreamed up by an ant. She had discovered that her antennae were neatly hinged so that they could be raised up and down and rotated. If she zipped up the side of the ink bottle

and dipped both antennae into the ink, then zoomed down on to the large piece of paper, she could drop dots of ink to form letters, thereby writing a message for Maud. This involved countless trips up and down the ink bottle in order to write anything that was big enough to read. In human

form this would have been impossible,
but an ant has limitless focused energy
and will carry on with any task until it
drops. Mildred wished that she could
somehow retain this extraordinary
sense of purpose to use during lessons
and exams once she was changed back
into herself! After twenty manic
minutes she had written

and decided that this was enough to
make Maud notice something odd.

She set about cutting the paper with her sharp ant jaws into a size that she could drag up on to Maud's bed. After several minutes of feeling her way up the bedclothes, she reached the lower slopes of Maud's face and began swatting her with the piece of paper. Maud didn't wake up, but every now and then scrabbled at her face and shouted in her sleep. Mildred valiantly continued scuttling out of the way, then flapping the paper against Maud's face – but apart from the occasional shout Maud remained fast asleep.

Next door, Enid heard Maud's voice and wondered if she was all right. Another shout echoed down the corridor and Enid could tell that it was her friend, half asleep and rambling, so she decided to go next door and wake her from whatever dream was upsetting her.

'Maudy,' whispered Enid, pushing open Maud's door and holding her candle aloft so that she could see around the room. 'Wake up, Maud, you're having a bad –' She stopped as she was confronted with the bizarre sight of a piece of paper flicking backwards and forwards against Maud's face, apparently all by itself.

'Maud! Wake up!' called Enid. 'There's something really weird going on!'

Maud woke up, rubbing her eyes, and Enid snatched the piece of paper and examined it in the candlelight.

'What's wrong, Enid?' cried Maud in alarm, propping herself up on her elbows. 'It's the middle of the night!'

'You were shouting in your sleep,' said Enid. 'I thought you were having a nightmare, but when I came in, this piece of paper was sort of flapping around your face like a moth or something; look, it's got writing on it.'

'What's it say?' asked Maud, screwing up her eyes against the candlelight.

'It says, "HELP NOT ANT". What on earth does *that* mean? *What's* "NOT ANT"?'

'Perhaps it means *an* ant,' said Maud.

'*What* ant, though?' asked Enid. 'Can *you* see an ant anywhere?'

They held up the candle and immediately saw the ant-Mildred, who had laboriously climbed off the bed, back on to the table, and carefully positioned herself in the middle of one of the sheets of white notepaper, where she knew she would be noticed. Maud and Enid brought the candle closer to the table so that they could see the ant and also the ink-splatters where it had splashed some of the drops while writing the note. It was obvious that this was the ant in question.

'If you're "NOT ANT",' said Enid, 'then what are you?'

The ant jumped up and down and twirled its feelers.

'Are you – a person?' asked Maud.

The ant jerked its antennae up and down like mini-cranes and turned round twice in a complete circle. Maud and Enid looked at each other with growing unease.

'You're not – Mildred?' asked Enid. 'You're not our friend Mildred Hubble?'

At this, the ant began capering about, nodding with its antennae, and zooming round and round in circles.

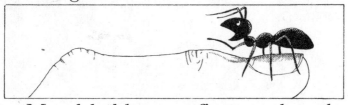

Maud held out a finger solemnly and the ant bustled on to it. 'Oh, Mildred,' said Maud. 'What on earth have you done *now*? Or did someone do this to you?'

The ant moved its antennae from side to side like a metronome and shook its head.

'Did *you* do it, then?' asked Maud.

Much nodding with the antennae.

'Well, then,' said Enid, 'why can't you change yourself back?'

The ant ran to the end of Maud's finger and obviously wanted to get down. Maud put her gently back on to the paper and watched as Mildred zipped up the side of the ink bottle and began running up and down with antennae drops of ink until she had written

'There's *two* l's in "spell",' said Enid helpfully.

'Don't be petty, Enid!' said Maud. 'It takes forever to write *anything* in ink drops. We can *see* it's "spell", clever-clogs! Let's find insect spells in *Spell Sessions Two* from last year. It's on the shelf by my bed. That would be more helpful than giving the poor ant a spelling lesson! I know Mildred was going to do insect spells for her summer-holiday project.'

They found the ant spell, complete with reversal.

'I don't know if this will work, Mil,' said Maud. 'But if I say the reversal spell out loud, perhaps you could try to concentrate on it and say it in "ant" in your head and it might just work. I'll keep saying it over and over with little pauses in between and hope you can remember it long enough. OK? Right, here goes.'

Maud intoned the reversal spell, then stopped while they both peered hopefully at the ant. Nothing happened. Enid read it out this time, then they stopped and waited again.

The ant did not move and they were wondering what to do next when the air began to vibrate and judder – as if a huge, invisible lorry was passing through the room – and suddenly Mildred was standing on the table in front of them in a burst of swirling smoke and stars. She leapt from the table at once.

'Come on, *quickly*, you two!' she said. 'We can't delay. What time is it?'

Enid consulted her watch. 'It's half past one,' she said. 'But why –'

'Oh *no*!' said Mildred. 'We've only got half an hour! They're all swarming in at two o'clock by the backyard gate. There's not a moment to lose!'

'Hang on, Mil!' exclaimed Enid, grabbing her arm. 'What on earth is this about? *Who's* swarming in at two o'clock? You'd better explain before we all go charging off somewhere in our pyjamas!'

Mildred managed a very fast, rather garbled explanation about Miss Granite really being Agatha and the plot to take over the school and how she had locked Mildred in the cupboard – which explained the ant transformation so she could sneak under the door and raise the alarm.

'Crumbs, Mil!' said Maud. 'We'd

better wake Miss Cackle at once.'

'Blow out the candle, Enid,' said Mildred. 'We'll have to be really quiet. Agatha is planning this like a battle campaign and she's absolutely ruthless.'

They snuffed out the candle, crept into the corridor and up to the teachers' rooms as fast as possible, which was quite difficult when they had to pause at every turn in case they bumped into Agatha.

As they approached the top corridor, where the headmistress had her bedroom, they saw Miss Cackle sneaking along towards her own door. Enid was just about to call out when Mildred grabbed her and clapped a hand over her mouth. She had seen, in the lantern light, that this person was holding a jam jar with leaves in it. Mildred caught Enid and Maud's gaze and pressed a finger to her lips as the door opened and the shadowy figure slipped inside.

'What's up, Mil?' whispered Maud, as soon as the door had closed. 'We need Miss Cackle to help us!'

'It isn't Miss Cackle!' said Mildred. 'It's Agatha. Don't forget, she looks *exactly* like Miss Cackle. She's got a jam jar, so I'll bet she's going to snail-ize her! But I can remember the snail transformation spell and if we're fast and very brave, we can get there first and turn the tables. Come on, *I*'ll fling the door open, *you* both jump on her and I'll do the snail spell. Let's go for it!'

CHAPTER SEVENTEEN

They flung the door open and saw Agatha poised with arm outstretched towards the sleeping Miss Cackle. Enid and Maud sprang across the room and hurled themselves on to her. They all went down in a mass of arms and legs, like a rugby scrum, as Mildred tried to get a clear zap at Agatha while chanting the snail spell.

Miss Cackle was now sitting up in bed, a look of complete astonishment on her face, as this amazing scene took place in front of her.

'What on earth are you girls doing?' she exclaimed, sounding furious.

'Can't explain yet, Miss Cackle!' said Mildred, delighted to find that only Enid and Maud were now on the floor and that a rather large snail was making for the open door. Mildred picked up the snail-Agatha and dropped her on to the bed of leaves in the jam jar. She handed the jar to Miss

Cackle. 'Look, Miss Cackle,' she explained. 'It's Agatha! She's been here all the time, disguised as Miss Granite. She was just about to snail-ize you. See, your name is on the jar. Her

coven of witches is arriving in –' she
glanced at Miss Cackle's wall clock –
'exactly fifteen minutes at the backyard
gate. We've got to head them off!'

'Good gracious me!' exclaimed
Miss Cackle. 'You mean my sister,
Agatha, has been right here under my
very nose all this time *masquerading* as
Miss Granite? She must have been
laughing up her sleeve at all of us; why
I even *hired* her against Miss
Hardbroom's advice – I'll never hear
the last of that! Come along, girls, let's
go down to the back gate and work
out a plan. We can leave my sister
here safely in the jar intended for me!'

'What are we going to *do*, Miss
Cackle?' asked Maud nervously, as
they arrived at the back gate at one
fifty, with ten minutes to spare. At that
very moment, the handle began to
turn and the gate creaked open.

'Jump on them!' yelled Mildred.

The three friends hurled themselves at the person coming through the gate and flung her to the ground. A beautiful black cat leapt yowling out of the way and a broomstick, carried by the person, snapped in half as they all collapsed on to the floor.

'What is the meaning of this?' thundered a terrifying voice they knew so well. 'Have you all lost your senses!'

It was Miss Hardbroom, home late from an unexpectedly difficult game of chess with Miss Pentangle – and, to make matters worse, Miss Pentangle had won.

Mildred and Enid sheepishly helped Miss Hardbroom to her feet, while Maud retrieved Miss Hardbroom's hat, which was squashed almost completely flat where everyone had fallen on it. Miss Hardbroom was so angry that she was emitting tiny sparks and puffs of purple smoke from her ears. She looked as if she might actually explode. The girls gazed across imploringly at Miss Cackle, who came to their rescue.

'Thank goodness it's you, Miss Hardbroom,' she said, dusting her down. 'Let me quickly explain to you that, in five minutes' time, we are yet *again* expecting an invasion of the school by a coven of evil witches, masterminded by my appalling sister, Agatha. You were quite right about Miss Granite's teaching qualities, Miss Hardbroom. In fact she is not a teacher at all, she is my evil twin sister in disguise. Fortunately, Mildred here discovered the plot to turn us all into snails. Mildred has already caught and snail-ized Agatha, who is upstairs, imprisoned in one of her own glass jars. The rest are arriving in precisely –' she looked at her watch – 'three minutes from now, expecting to be met by Agatha. I really can't quite think how to deal with this in such a short space of time.'

Miss Hardbroom took all this in her stride immediately, as if it was quite normal to be greeted by such an astonishing story at two o'clock in the morning.

'It's obvious what to do, Miss Cackle,' she said, taking the helm at once. 'The rest of Agatha's witches will be expecting Agatha to let them in. As you look *exactly* like your sister, just let them in – in a confident way. Tell them to wait outside and you will let them in one by one. Mildred can turn them into snails as they come in. Do you think you're up to a mass snail-in, Mildred?'

'It's my best spell, Miss Hardbroom,' said Mildred. 'I can do ants now too,' she added proudly.

'What have ants got to do with it?' snapped Miss Hardbroom. 'Just concentrate on snails, Mildred. We don't want to find an ants' nest under the floorboards.'

The hall clock struck two, and a light tap was heard on the back door. The girls' hearts were thumping as they stood in the shadows and watched Miss Cackle open the door. 'One at a time, ladies,' she whispered into the yard, as she ushered the first witch inside.

CHAPTER EIGHTEEN

By three o'clock, Miss Hardbroom, Miss Cackle and their three exhausted pupils were all up in Miss Cackle's room, contemplating several shoeboxes full of the entire coven, except for one jam jar, which contained Agatha, now sulking under the leaves.

Mildred had rescued Tabby from his cat-basket prison in the impostor's room and was holding him very gently.

'Let's all have a nice cup of tea!' said Miss Cackle. 'I really think we deserve one after such a ghastly night – especially Mildred here. I know that she does have her moments of – unruliness, Miss Hardbroom, but she also does have quite an extraordinary knack of being in the right place at the right time – especially when it comes to my sister! No wonder Agatha locked her in the airing cupboard as fast as possible!'

Miss Hardbroom took Mildred's arm and pulled her towards the wall lantern.

'What are all these little black specks on your face?' she said, peering at Mildred, who shrank back nervously. 'You look as if someone's sprayed ink all over you.'

'I think it was from when I was an ant, Miss Hardbroom,' said Mildred.

'An *ant*?' said Miss Hardbroom. 'What *is* all this about ants, Mildred?'

'Never mind,' soothed Miss Cackle. 'It's a long story and we're all tired out. We'll have to find a new teacher for Form Three first thing tomorrow. Actually, I've just received a late application from a Miss Mould, who sounds promising; she teaches art and ceramics, as well as basic potions and advanced flying. What do you think, Miss Hardbroom?'

'I think she sounds a *possible*, Miss Cackle,' agreed Miss Hardbroom. 'But I think she *might* be best for my Year Twos. They're a quiet bunch this year and I can see that Form Three would benefit from some firm guidance after such a dreadful start to the term.'

'An excellent idea, Miss Hardbroom.' Miss Cackle beamed. 'I'm sure the girls would be most relieved to be back in your care for a third year – wouldn't you, girls?'

The girls looked stunned and didn't know what to say.

'That's settled, then,' said Miss Cackle. 'Off to bed now, girls, and thank you for all your hard work.'

The three friends trooped downstairs together.

'I have to hand it to you, Milly,' said Maud with a smile. 'Things are never boring when you're around! I don't know why H.B. calls you the Worst Witch. I think she ought to create a special award just for you!'

'You're unique!' laughed Enid. 'The one and only, never-to-be-repeated Mildred Hubble – always gets *out* of trouble, whatever it is!'

'I know it sounds a bit weird,' said Mildred, draping Tabby over her shoulder and smoothing the fur between his ears, 'but I think it might actually be quite *comforting* to have Miss Hardbroom bossing us all around again. More *normal*, if you know what I mean.'

Maud agreed heartily. 'I know *just* what you mean, Mil,' she said. 'I have to admit that I was almost pining for some law and order over the last few days!'

Miss Hardbroom materialized with a whoosh at the entrance to the Form Three bedrooms.

'And I've missed you too,' she said, with an *almost* friendly smile. 'You may be hard work, Form Three, but you certainly come up with some *very* interesting results!'

This brief flicker of friendliness was gone in a second. 'Now then, into your rooms, lights out and asleep in two minutes,' she barked, 'and no more talking.'

155

Mildred dived under the covers and settled Tabby in his usual position on her chest. To her delight, he started to purr and butt her hand so that she could go on smoothing his head, just the way he liked, and before long the two of them were so fast asleep that they didn't even hear the bats come in from their night's hunting.